W9-BOA-232

To Humzah, my inspiration to start writing;
to Mariam, whose creativity inspires me daily; and
to Zayd, who brings joy to everything — *R. O. G.*

To my wonderful nephews and nieces who
make me laugh every day — *M. M.*

Hana's HUNDREDS of Hijabs

words by Razeena Omar Gutta   art by Manal Mirza

Barefoot Books
Step inside a story

Hana has hundreds of hijabs. She collects them wherever she goes, from secondhand shops and shopping malls, to her cousins' closets and online sales. She even upcycles her mama's old skirts!

Her drawers are overflowing with accessories too — sparkling, glimmering, beaded. She's found her prized pieces among her grandmother's jewels and at Aunty Huda's hair salon, where she helps out after school.

Her hijab is always styled magnificently . . .
but aside from having more hijabs than she can
possibly wear, she has one peculiar problem.

Once Hana places the first jewel, knot or layer on her hijab, she cannot stop! Her fingers flow with talent, decorating to be fancier and more flamboyant.

This means she is often overdressed
(with exquisite attention to detail),
often late (hijab styling does take
time), and her hijabs often take over
the entire house.

She tries limiting herself to only
one style but she can never stick to it!

She tries packing her jewels away, but still finds a way to make everything hijab-able.

She donates some . . . but still has more than she can manage. She's still tempted to keep styling. Hana is an artist and her hijab is her canvas.

Her friends have no ideas to help her — only questions. Hana is their go-to creativity consultant and her hijabs sparkle with joy, just like her.

Her teacher is usually encouraging.

You're so original! Maybe try waking up a little earlier so you're not running late.

But Hana knows that the more time she has, the more styling she can do.

Hana loves her hijab. She knows it's important and she feels special when she wears it, just like so many strong women she admires, especially Mama.

Her mama loves to watch Hana style her hijab.

Hana, you're ingenious!

But Hana knows Mama gets annoyed when her stuff clutters every room.

How can she share her hijab-fabulous ideas without always being late or leaving a mess behind her?

While Hana helps out at Aunty Huda's salon, she observes carefully.

The customers always love their new hairstyles.

Hana hatches a hijab-tastic idea.

Hana hauls her hijab supplies over to
Aunty Huda's salon. Boxes full of jewels and
rhinestones are stacked like a tower. A rainbow
of fabrics flows over the sides. Her collection
practically glows from the pavement.

She crafts a sign (covered in jewels,
of course) and puts it outside.

HAPHAZARD
HIJAB NO MORE!

Let Hana Hijabi fix
your failing fashion
and coordinate your
combinations.

*Also styling hats, headpieces
and hair accessories.*

Appointments available

When word gets out, Hana
can't keep up with demand.

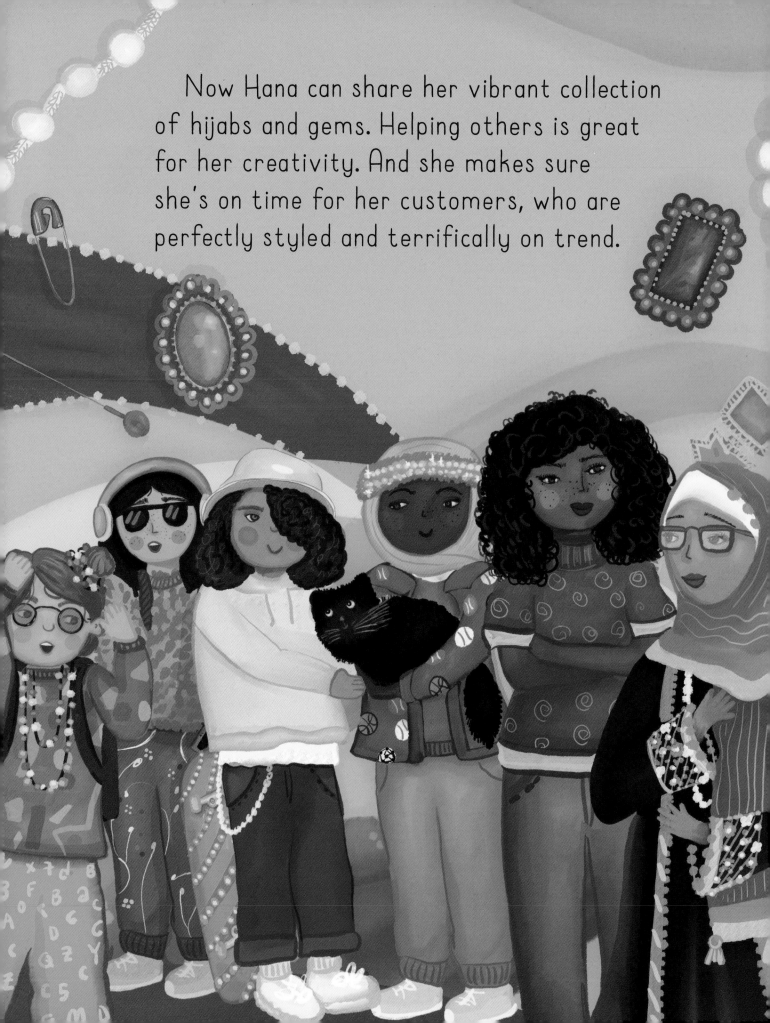

Now Hana can share her vibrant collection of hijabs and gems. Helping others is great for her creativity. And she makes sure she's on time for her customers, who are perfectly styled and terrifically on trend.

As people exit the salon after Hana's sparkly styling service, they wear an equally sparkly smile on their faces. And Hana is happiest of all.

Salaam! I'm Hana and I'm nine. I don't have to wear the hijab yet, but I love how it makes me look and feel. Many Muslim women wear it as part of our obedience and devotion to God. Many women of faith cover their hair, including some Christian nuns, Orthodox Jews, Sikhs and Hindus. If you'd like to know more about hijab in Islam, you can visit *https://yaqeeninstitute.org/tag/hijab*.

Meet the Author and Illustrator!

If Hana were to design your hijab, what would it look like?

Razeena, author

Manal, illustrator

What does hijab mean to you?

Razeena: Hijab means fulfilling my obligation as a Muslim woman. It means being strong in a world that doesn't always value my religion and it means being true to myself and my beliefs.

Manal: Hijab can be seen as just a cloth that covers your hair, but its meaning is much greater. It means being modest, being strong in character and in faith. It means to stand up for yourself and represent a whole religion.

What kinds of hijabs do you like?

Razeena: Depends on my mood — sometimes bright, sometimes neutral. I'm not a big fan of printed hijabs at the moment.

Manal: The hijab I wear most often is black and olive.

Do you ever have bad hijab days?

Razeena: Yes! Sometimes it just doesn't stay in place or look the way I want it to look.

Manal: Yes, of course!

What hijab style do you like best?

Razeena: Softly draped, with minimal pins.

Manal: A soft material that is casually wrapped around.

How do you like to accessorize?

Razeena: I don't really accessorize but after seeing Hana's artistry I think I should!

Manal: I don't usually use hijab accessories, but I love wearing earrings and a long necklace.

Barefoot Books, 23 Bradford Street, 2nd Floor, Concord, MA 01742
29/30 Fitzroy Square, London, W1T 6LQ

Text copyright © 2022 by Razeena Omar Gutta. Illustrations copyright © 2022 by Manal Mirza. The moral rights of Razeena Omar Gutta and Manal Mirza have been asserted

Graphic design by Elizabeth Jayasekera, Barefoot Books
Edited and art directed by Autumn Allen and Lisa Rosinsky, Barefoot Books
Reproduction by Bright Arts, Hong Kong. Printed in Malaysia

This book was typeset in Catalina Clemente, Delivery Note, Gorditas and Sweet Apricot. The illustrations were created digitally using Procreate

Hardback ISBN 978-1-64686-620-5
Paperback ISBN 978-1-64686-621-2
E-book ISBN 978-1-64686-702-8

British Cataloguing-in-Publication Data: a catalogue record for this book is available from the British Library

Library of Congress Cataloging-in-Publication Data is available under LCCN 2022935464

1 3 5 7 9 8 6 4 2

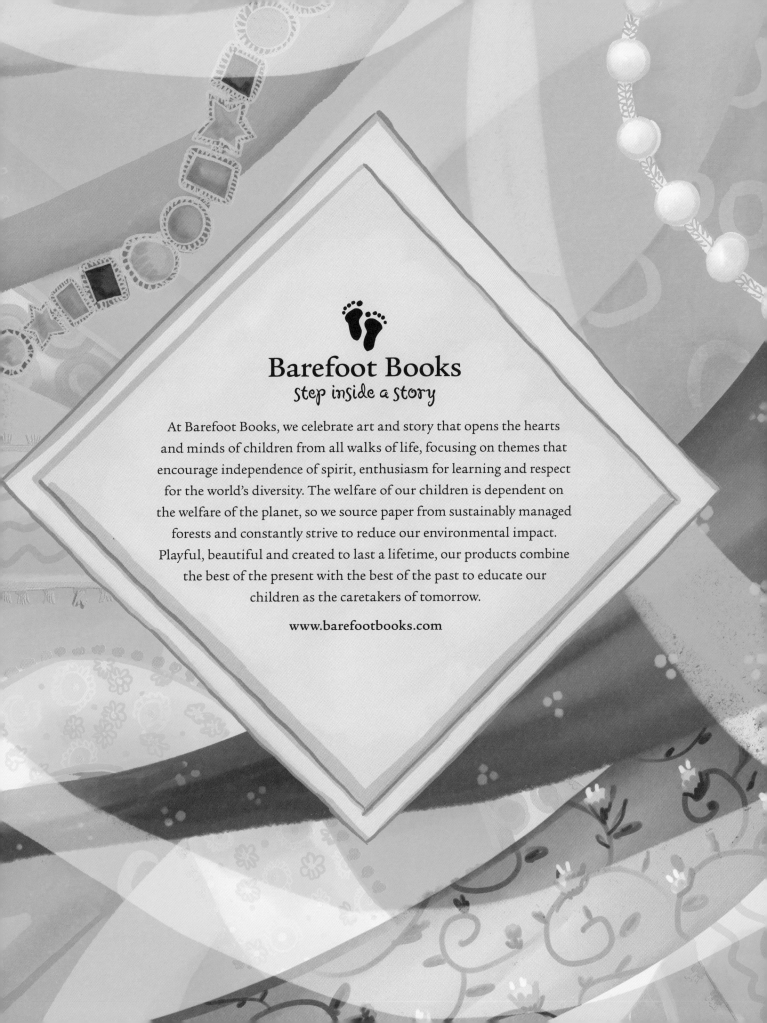

Barefoot Books
step inside a story

At Barefoot Books, we celebrate art and story that opens the hearts and minds of children from all walks of life, focusing on themes that encourage independence of spirit, enthusiasm for learning and respect for the world's diversity. The welfare of our children is dependent on the welfare of the planet, so we source paper from sustainably managed forests and constantly strive to reduce our environmental impact. Playful, beautiful and created to last a lifetime, our products combine the best of the present with the best of the past to educate our children as the caretakers of tomorrow.

www.barefootbooks.com

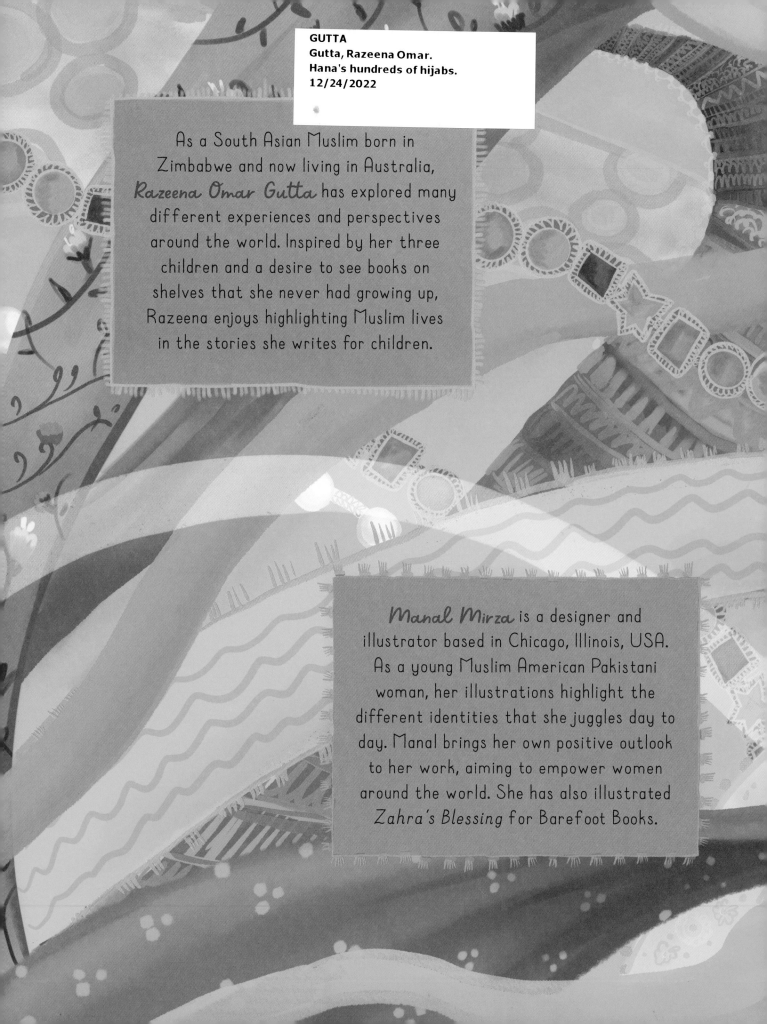

As a South Asian Muslim born in Zimbabwe and now living in Australia, *Razeena Omar Gutta* has explored many different experiences and perspectives around the world. Inspired by her three children and a desire to see books on shelves that she never had growing up, Razeena enjoys highlighting Muslim lives in the stories she writes for children.

Manal Mirza is a designer and illustrator based in Chicago, Illinois, USA. As a young Muslim American Pakistani woman, her illustrations highlight the different identities that she juggles day to day. Manal brings her own positive outlook to her work, aiming to empower women around the world. She has also illustrated *Zahra's Blessing* for Barefoot Books.